W9-CDB-458

# *Naming the Cat*

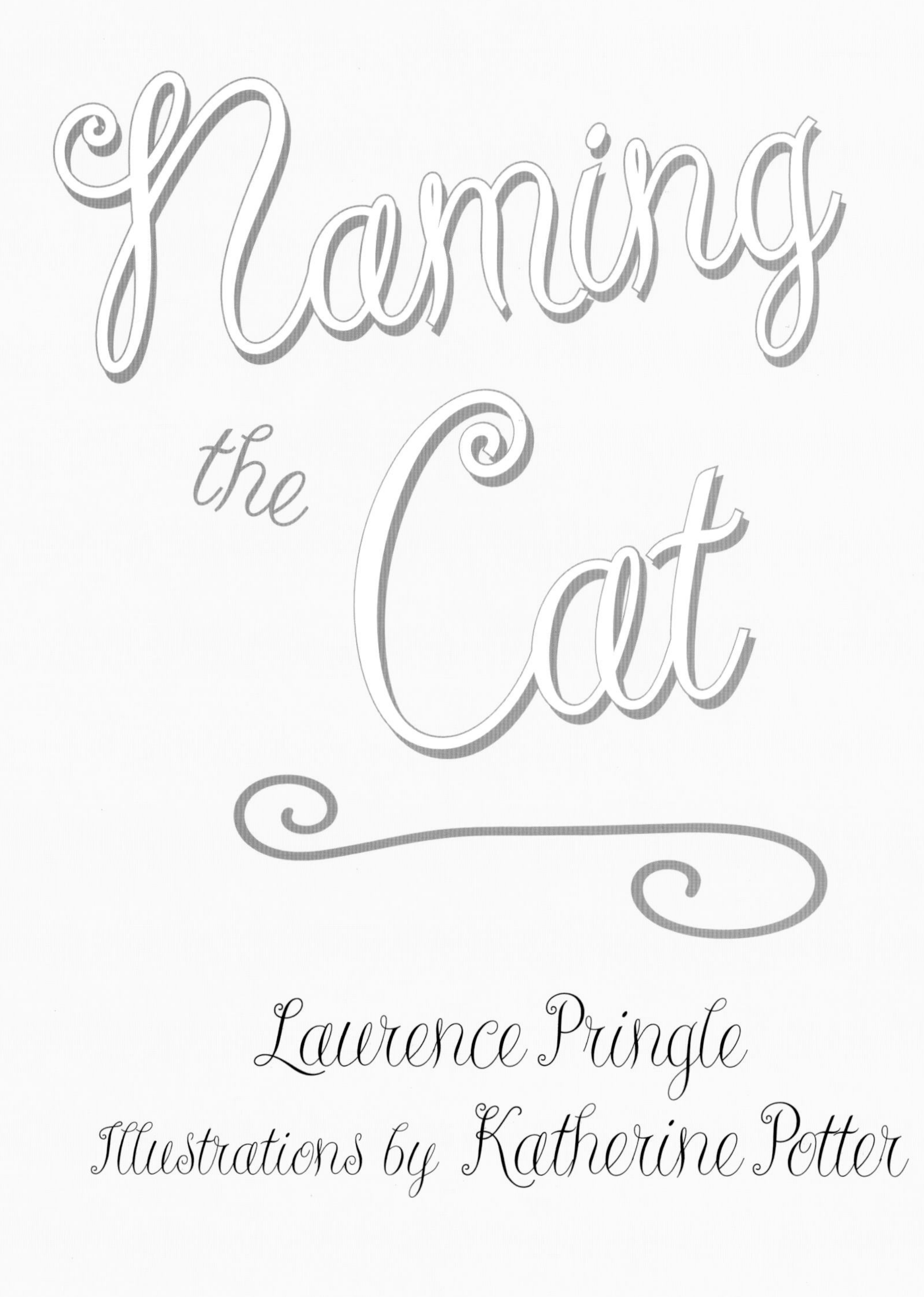

# Naming the Cat

Laurence Pringle

Illustrations by Katherine Potter

Walker and Company New York

*For Sylvester, Sabrina, Cricket, and especially for Willow, whose naming inspired this story.*
*—L. P.*

*To John*
*—K. P.*



First published in the United States of America in 1997 by Walker Publishing Company, Inc.

Published simultaneously in Canada by Thomas Allen & Son Canada, Limited, Markham, Ontario

Library of Congress Cataloging-in-Publication Data
Pringle, Laurence P.
Naming the cat/Laurence Pringle; illustrations by Katherine Potter.
p. cm.
Summary: A family considers many possibilities before coming up with a name that is just right for the cat that has come to live with them.
ISBN 0-8027-8621-9 (hc).—ISBN 0-8027-8622-7 (rein)
[1. Cats—Fiction. 2. Names, Personal—Fiction.] I. Potter, Katherine, ill. II. Title.
PZ7.P93647Nam 1997
[E]—dc21 97-443
CIP
AC

Book design by Janet Pedersen

PRINTED IN HONG KONG
2 4 6 8 10 9 7 5 3 1

One morning, a cat came calling at our back door.

We gave him some milk in a saucer. He asked for seconds. He was more curious than afraid, walking from room to room, exploring.

He rubbed his body against chair legs and our legs. Then he snuggled in a lap and took a nap.

“Is anyone missing a cat?” we asked all over the neighborhood. The cat seemed to be ours to keep.

"What shall we name the cat?" Mom asked.

"Cinderella," my sister suggested.

"That's a girl's name," said Mom, "and this is a boy cat."

We all began to suggest names for the cat.

We could not agree on a name. "That's okay," said Dad. "We can call him Cat or Kitty for a while. Sooner or later, one name will seem just right."

Mom was impatient. She wanted to name the cat NOW. "Let's just look at him," she urged, "and name what you see."

We still could not agree on one name. "Maybe," Dad said, "the cat will do something that will tell us his name."

Meanwhile, the cat made himself at home. He was young and frisky. One day he tried to catch a fly as it buzzed around the house. Leaping up to catch it, the cat knocked a glass vase off the table. But the vase fell onto a chair cushion and didn't break.

Mother scooped up the cat and stroked its head. "You are a lucky cat," she said.

That night Dad offered a couple of new names. He was a scientist, and had to explain them. "Orca," Dad suggested. "That's a killer whale, black on top and white below, just like our kitty."

"Or how about Nimbus, a dark rain cloud?"

Mom, who was a teacher, said, "I would rather call the cat Nimble, which means quick and agile, than name it after a rain cloud."

The cat did not seem to mind being nameless. Sometimes we let him explore outside near the house. He chased windblown leaves and caught insects to eat. When we called "Kitty, Kitty, Kitty," he came to the door, happy to return home.

One day I had just let the cat outdoors when a big dog came into the yard. The dog saw the cat, growled, and ran toward it.

I opened the door and the cat scooted in. “You were lucky I was still by the door,” I told the cat.

Macavity Shimbleshanks

For Grandma's birthday we went to the theater. We saw the play *Cats*, and heard some extraordinary names.

They did not fit our cat.

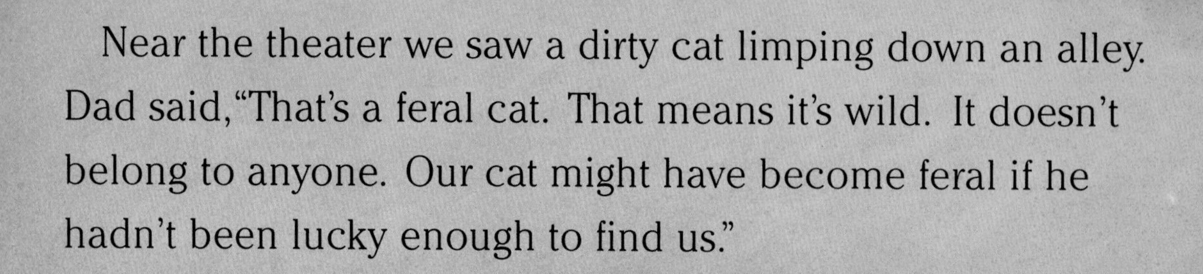

Near the theater we saw a dirty cat limping down an alley. Dad said, "That's a feral cat. That means it's wild. It doesn't belong to anyone. Our cat might have become feral if he hadn't been lucky enough to find us."

My teacher said that our cat could visit my class for a while if he stayed in his cat carrier. The kids in the class had plenty of names for him.

Muffin Mellow Splinter
COMFY CAT

Everyone wanted to pet the cat, so I opened the door of the carrier a bit. Kids reached in. Suddenly the cat bolted out and began to race around the room. He was scared. Everybody, including Miss Boniello, yelled in excitement. The cat dashed from under a desk and leaped away from all the noise . . . right out the window.

He fell down, down, down. His body twisted and turned until he straightened out and landed on his feet in the soft sand of the playground.

He sat there shaking until I raced down to pick him up. I gave him a gentle hug and he began to purr. He wasn't hurt. "Wow," I said, "you sure are lucky."

And that is how our cat was named.